DIANA WOLKSTEIN

A folk tale from Haiti in the Caribbean

Illustrated by Tracy Fennell

BBC/LONGMAN

Owl thought he was very ugly. But one evening he met a girl and talked with her and she liked him. "If it had been day," Owl thought, "and she had seen my face, she never would have liked me." But still she had liked him.

So Owl went to her house the next night. And the next. And the night after that. Every evening he would arrive at the girl's house at seven, and they would sit outside on the porch steps, talking together politely.

Then one evening after Owl had left, the girl's mother said to her, "Why doesn't your fiancé come and visit you during the day?"

"But Mama, he's explained that to me. He works during the day. Then he must go home and change and he can't get here before seven."

"Still, I would like to see his face before the marriage," the mother said. "Let's invite him to our house for a dance, this Sunday afternoon. Surely, he doesn't work on Sunday."

Owl was very pleased with the invitation: a dance in his honour. But he was also very frightened. He told his cousin, Rooster, about the girl and asked him to accompany him to the dance. But that Sunday afternoon, as Owl and Rooster were riding on their horses to the dance, Owl glanced over at Rooster. Rooster held himself with such assurance, he was so elegantly and fashionably dressed, that Owl imagined the girl seeing the two of them and was filled with shame.

"I can't go on," he choked. "You go and tell them I've had an accident and I'll be there later."

Rooster rode to the dance. "Tsk tsk, poor Owl," he explained. "He has had an accident, and he has asked me to let you know that he will be here later."

When it was quite dark, Owl tied his horse a good distance from the dance and stumbled up to the porch steps.

“Pssst,” he whispered to a young man sitting on the steps. “Is Rooster here?”

“Well now, I don’t know.”

“Go and look. Tell him a friend is waiting for him by the mapou tree.”

Rooster came out. "OWL!"

"Shhhhhh--"

"Owl!"

"Shhh--"

"Owl, what are you wearing over your head – I mean your face?"

"It's a hat. Haven't you ever seen a hat before? Look, tell them anything. Tell them I scratched my eyes on a branch as I was riding here and the light – even the light from a lamp – hurts them. And you must be certain to watch for the day for me, and to crow as soon as you see the light, so we can leave."

"Yes, yes," Rooster said. "Come in and I shall introduce you to the girl's relatives."

Rooster introduced Owl to everyone, explaining Owl's predicament. Owl went around shaking hands, his hat hung down almost completely covering his face. Owl then tried to retreat into a corner, but the girl came over.

"Come into the yard and let's dance," she said.

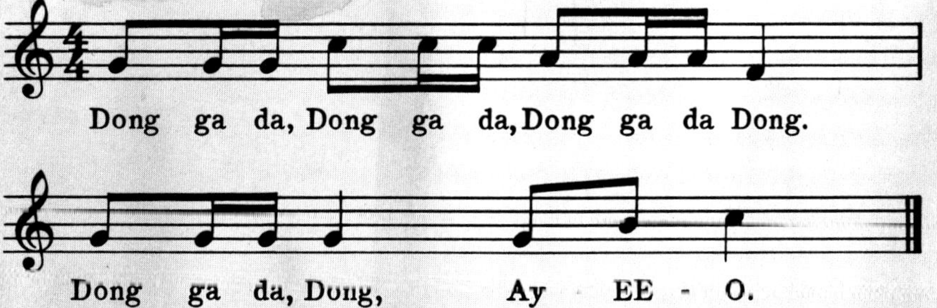

Owl danced. And Owl could dance well. The girl was proud of Owl. Even if he wore his hat strangely and had sensitive eyes, he *could* dance.

Dong ga da, Dong ga da, Dong ga da, Dong.
Dong ga da, Dong. Ay EE O.

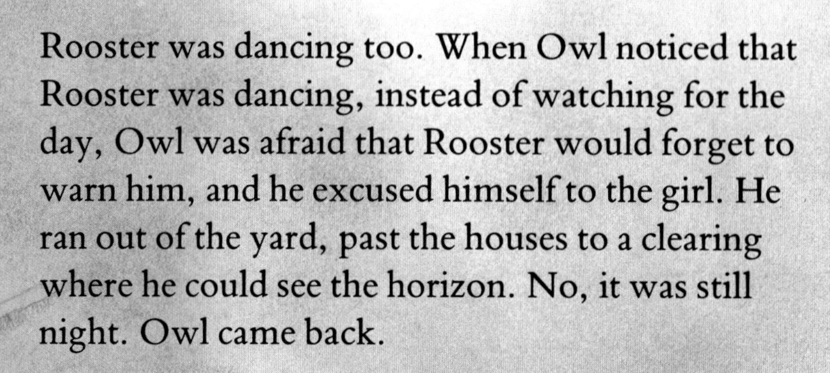

Rooster was dancing too. When Owl noticed that Rooster was dancing, instead of watching for the day, Owl was afraid that Rooster would forget to warn him, and he excused himself to the girl. He ran out of the yard, past the houses to a clearing where he could see the horizon. No, it was still night. Owl came back.

Dong ga da, Dong ga da, Dong ga da, Dong.
Dong ga da, Dong. Ay-EE-O.

Owl motioned to Rooster, but Rooster was lost in the dance. Owl excused himself again to the girl, ran to the clearing; no, it was still night. Owl returned.

Dong ga da, Dog ga da, Dong ga da, Dong.
Dong ga da, Dong. Ay-EE-O.

Owl tried to excuse himself again, but the girl held on to him. "Yes, stay with me," she said. And so they danced and danced and danced.

Dong ga da, Dong ga da, Dong ga da, Dong.
Dong ga da, Dong. Ay-EE-O.

The sun moved up in the sky, higher and higher,
until it filled the house and the yard with light.

"Now – let us see your fiancé's face!" the mother said.

"*Kokioko!*" Rooster crowed.

And before Owl could hide, she reached out and pulled the hat from his face.

"MY EYES!" Owl cried, and covering his face with his hands, he ran for his horse.

"Wait, Owl!" the girl called.

"*Kokioko!*" Rooster crowed.

"Wait, Owl, wait."

And as Owl put his hands down to untie his horse, the girl saw his face. It was striking and fierce, and the girl thought it was the most handsome face she had ever seen.

"Owl –"

But Owl was already on his horse, riding away, farther and farther away.

Owl never came back.

The girl waited. Then she married Rooster. She was happy, except sometimes in the morning when Rooster would crow "Kokioko-o-o."

Then she would think about Owl and wonder where he was.

Other titles in this series

Isn't my name magical? Poems by James Berry
Sea tongue by Kevin Crossley-Holland
Trellie the troog by Douglas Hill
The porcelain man by Richard Kennedy
Caruso's cool cats by Dick King-Smith
Cap o' Rushes by Alison Lurie
Dare's secret pony by Emma Tennant

Series consultants: Myra Barrs and Sue Ellis, Director and Deputy Director of the Centre for Learning in Primary Education (Southwark).

The series accompanies the BBC School Radio series, *Listening and Reading* on Radio 5 Medium Wave.

Dedicated to Joan Higbee Bodger Mercer

Published by BBC Educational Publishing and Longman Group UK Limited

BBC Educational Publishing
a division of
BBC Enterprises Limited
Woodlands
80 Wood Lane
London W12 0TT

Longman Group UK Limited
Longman House
Burnt Mill
Harlow
Essex CM20 2JE
England and associated
companies throughout the world

First published in New York in 1980 in 'The Magic Orange Tree and other Haitian folktales; collected by Diana Wolkstein' by Schocken Books

Series editor Joan Griffiths
Cover and book design by
Cathy May
(school edition) ISBN 0 582 06231 4
(trade edition) ISBN 0 563 34784 8

Set in 14/18 Bembo Roman
Typeset by Goodfellow and Egan
Text and cover origination by
Dot Gradations
Printed and bound by Cambus Litho